KAYLEE MILLER

A
Guiding
Light
in the
Forest

KAYLEE MILLER

A Guiding Light in the Forest

A Guiding Light in the Forest

Copyright © 2023 by Kaylee Miller

First Edition

Hardcover ISBN: 979-8-8229-1279-3

Paperback ISBN: 979-8-8229-1280-9

Dedication

For O & J.

In the forest, there stood a tree. The tree was tall with strong branches resembling outstretched arms giving a big hug.

The forest animals loved the tree and visited it often. Some even stayed, making the tree their home.

One day the tree felt unwell. Its roots had stiffened, and the bark on its trunk began to flake. The tree's bright green leaves wilted and lost their vibrant color. Its branches were weak, sagging toward the ground in a frown. Why was the tree so sick?

Soon after the tree became ill, its shriveled leaves fell off one by one. The wind blew, carrying the leaves toward the sky. They eventually landed, forming piles around the tree's trunk.

HEALTHY
TREES

Season changes would come and go, and the tree knew that once an autumn chill was in the air, its leaves would fall and winter would be near, but summer had barely started. This is not how the tree expected to look or feel on a warm summer day. Would the forest animals leave to search for new homes in a healthier tree?

A little boy named Owen lived with his family at the edge of the forest. He loved animals and enjoyed spending time with the tree. He would sit in the shade beneath its branches, telling the tree all about the treasures he found while walking through the forest.

Owen and the forest animals could see that the tree was going through a tough time. The forest animals had never cared for a sick friend before and were unsure of what to do. They asked Owen if he had ever known anyone who was sick, and he said, "Yes, I have." They listened as he told them about how he felt when someone he loved was ill.

"Our feelings aren't always easy to understand when a loved one is sick," he explained. "You may be faced with battling an illness and have emotions that are hard to put into words. It is all right to not know how to tell someone how you are feeling. "I felt scared, sad, and angry all at the same time," Owen told the forest animals.

"When moments seemed uncertain and beyond my control, I felt better after I talked about them, even if what I said didn't come out quite like I wanted it to." The forest animals knew then just what Owen was talking about, and off they went to search for things to brighten the tree's day.

Owen brought soft, comforting blankets and a stack of his favorite books from home. He and the forest animals took turns telling jokes and reading stories to the tree. They didn't want the tree to feel alone, and they reassured their friend that trees are mighty and resilient. They encouraged the tree to rest and take it one day at a time, since being sick can make you extra tired.

The days were getting hotter. Owen and the forest animals couldn't remember the last time they'd played in the rain or splashed in a puddle. "I know why the tree is sick!" Owen exclaimed. The tree wasn't getting enough water, and that explained the changes it was experiencing. Too little water kept the tree from staying healthy. They needed to find water for the tree right away!

There was a waterfall close by. The forest animals put buckets into Owen's wagon and went to collect water.

Once their buckets were filled, they hurried back to the tree. They dumped water on the tree's roots and trunk. Birds came with watering cans and poured water onto the tree's branches. The water was cool, and the tree's bark soaked it in as if it were taking a long drink.

The forest animals stayed by the tree's side. The much-needed water mended the tree's damaged pieces. Its roots grew deeper into the soft ground. Its dry bark stopped flaking, and its weary branches were getting stronger. Buds emerged and soon sprouted tiny green leaves. They made sure the tree had enough water for the rest of the summer.

The forest animals had been very worried about the tree. Owen said that they each had something very special within them: A guiding light during difficult times.

Did you know that you have those same special things inside of you? If you are struggling, close your eyes and think of the forest animals. Wherever you are, they'll be there for you when you need them most. They will give you their special qualities, and soon you will find your own.

Hope

Love

Strength

Bravery

The bear is brave. When you are fearful, the bear will give you bravery. The deer is strong. When you feel weak, the deer will give you strength. The rabbit symbolizes hope. When you wish for healthy days ahead, the rabbit will give you hope. Love is healing. You are loved by all the forest animals, and you have more love to give than your heart can hold. That is an incredible amount of healing!

When you open your eyes, can you feel yourself becoming braver, stronger, and filled with hope and love? You are a friend to lean on, ready to conquer sickness head-on!

If your loved one is ill, they may have trouble finding the special things they have inside of them too. Can you help them like Owen and the forest animals found water for the tree? Ask them to close their eyes and tell them all about the forest animals.

Bravery, strength, hope, and love can be found in the most unexpected places. Search for joy around every corner.

That joy will stay with you and bring you comfort on the days when happiness is hiding.